Little Lion

Written by Dyan Beyer

Illustrated by Carolee Carrara

To order additional copies of this book, contact:
Xlibris
844-714-8691
www.Xlibris.com
Orders@Xlibris.com

ISBN:	Softcover	978-1-6698-1206-7
	Hardcover	978-1-6698-1296-8
	EBook	978-1-6698-1205-0

Print information available on the last page

Rev. date: 02/23/2022

For our newest grandson, Creed Henry. You were already loved before you were born and I couldn't wait to love you in person!

Books by Dyan Beyer

Under Angels' Wings

Baby Boy Bear

Baby Grace Is Here!

Baby Needs Pants

Samuel 1:27: "For this child we have prayed."

Psalms 34:10: "Even strong young lions sometimes go hungry but those who trust in the Lord, will lack no good thing."

nce upon a time there was a little boy, named Creed Henry, who wanted a puppy. But because he was young his mom and dad said he would have to wait until he was older to get a puppy.

"Why?" Asked Creed Henry.

"Well, because a puppy is a lot of work. A dog needs to be fed, walked, groomed, played with and most of all you have to take time to train a puppy," said Mommy and Daddy.

"I can do all of that! Really I can! I promise...please! Please can I get a puppy?" The little boy pleaded.

Mommy and Daddy were still not convinced that Creed Henry was old enough to take on that responsibility.

"I know you mean well but we still think it is not the right time for you to have a puppy."

Creed Henry was very sad and after making a few more attempts at changing Mommy and Daddy's mind, he gave up and went to his room. He prayed to God that his mom and dad would let him get a puppy soon.

"Dear Lord, I know I am a little boy but I know I can take care of a puppy! I will be loving and kind to my puppy. I will always remember to feed, walk and play with my little dog. If there is something I left out, please forgive me. All creatures are from you, so if you think I will be good to your creation, please let me have a puppy! Thank you, God!...Oh, and Amen!"

He hugged, Ruff, his stuffed animal puppy as he laid on his bed. Big tears slid down the boys cheeks.

"I know I can do all of the things Mommy and Daddy talked about. I know I can!"

Creed Henry pulled Ruff close and asked, "Don't I take good care of you, Ruff? Don't I play with you and take you on walks with me? Don't I make sure you are safely tucked into bed with me at night?"

The little boy knew it was silly to talk to something that wasn't real but it made him feel better.

"I love you, Ruff and if I had a real puppy I would love him too! But don't worry, I would still play with you and love you...it's just that a real puppy would be able to play with ME. He would run after a ball and bring it back to me. He would bark to keep me safe. He would eat food when I fed him. Most of all he would be my pal...I sure do wish you were real, Ruff. I really do...really..." said Creed Henry yawning.

Suddenly the stuffed animal gave a little yelp! Creed Henry jumped up not sure of what he just heard. "Yelp...!"

There it was again! The boy ran to window looking to see if there was a puppy outside. But when he heard the "Yelp" again, it was coming from Ruff!

Creed Henry slowly walked back to his bed and picked up Ruff. Looking into the stuffed animal's face he asked, "Did you make that sound?"

"Yep, who else is in here with us?" Ruff asked smiling.

"What! You can talk?...Are you real?"

"Course I am little boy! I was just waiting for you to ask me to play with you."

Creed Henry looked up, "Thank you, God!"

"God always answers your prayers when the time is right," Ruff said.

"OH WOW! You are real...can you chase a ball? Can you take a walk with me? And I can feed you? Can you give me your paw? Can I…"

"Slow down a bit, boy! I can do all of those things and more. I do tricks as well!"

The little boy, Creed Henry, was so happy he started jumping up and down squeezing Ruff.

"Not so tight, you're crushing me..."

"I'm sorry boy..."

"Oh, and I am not a boy. I'm a girl!"

"That's fine with me, as long as you are a real puppy!"

"Well I'm talking and moving so I guess I am real!"

"Are you hungry?" Creed Henry asked Ruff.

"Always! I haven't had a good steak in years!" Ruff said licking his lips.

"Steak?...I don't think I can get you that but I can get you some scraps from dinner tonight!"

"Better than what I have been eating..."

"What have you been eating?" Asked Creed Henry.

"Nothing! That's why it's better!" Ruff answered with a smile.

The little boy and Ruff laughed and played all afternoon together. When Mommy and Daddy called Creed Henry for dinner, he didn't want to leave his newfound friend.

"Go, boy, I'm starving, bring me back some food."

"Okay, I will!" Creed Henry said before running down to dinner.

When Creed Henry entered into the kitchen, Mommy and Daddy seemed like they were in a serious discussion.

"Oh, there you are. Come sit down. Your Mom and I have been thinking about allowing you to have a puppy. That's if you will take care..." the boy didn't allow his dad to finish what he was saying.

"A PUPPY! REALLY?" Creed Henry shouted out in surprise.

"Well, there will be some rules and responsibilities that go along with that." Mommy added.

"I will do anything....but wait...I already have a..." the boy quickly stopped talking. Creed Henry suddenly realized that he did have a real puppy. He had Ruff, up in his room!

"You already have what?" asked Daddy.

Creed Henry didn't know what to say or how to answer his dad's question. He wasn't sure if Ruff wanted everyone to know he was real.

"Are you okay?" Asked Mommy.

"Yes, I am...I just can't believe you are letting me get another... I mean, letting me get a puppy!"

"Tomorrow we will go to Mr. Chinny Chin Chin Puppy Store and see what he has," said Daddy.

Dog food
PET SUPPLIES
Puppy Chow

The next morning, Creed Henry and his parents went to the Mr. Chinny Chin Chin Puppy Store to pick out a puppy. He was very excited and thought the new puppy would be great company for Ruff. He had discussed the new puppy with her last night and Ruff welcomed the idea.

When they arrived the next morning, Mr. Chinny Chin Chin was holding a cute little black puppy in his arms.

"Hello Mr. Chinny Chin Chin. We are looking for a puppy for Creed Henry," said Mommy.

"Well, I have plenty of pups. What kind are you looking for?" Mr. Chinny Chin Chin asked.

"What kind of puppy would you like, Creed Henry? Daddy asked.

Creed Henry had wanted a puppy for so long but never thought about what kind of puppy he would choose.

"I don't know, Daddy. I guess a pup that will play with me and that will love me."

Mr. Chinny Chin Chin quickly replied, "I think we can find one like that, come with me."

Following Mr. Chinny Chin Chin, they walked to the back of the puppy store. There were all types of puppies playing together. They started jumping and barking once they saw Creed Henry. He looked at all the pups and wanted all of them!

But there was one little puppy who kept coming over to Creed Henry and biting at his shoelaces. When the little boy reached down to pet him, the puppy jumped on top of Creed Henry causing him to tumble over. The puppy showed his affection by licking Creed Henry's face!

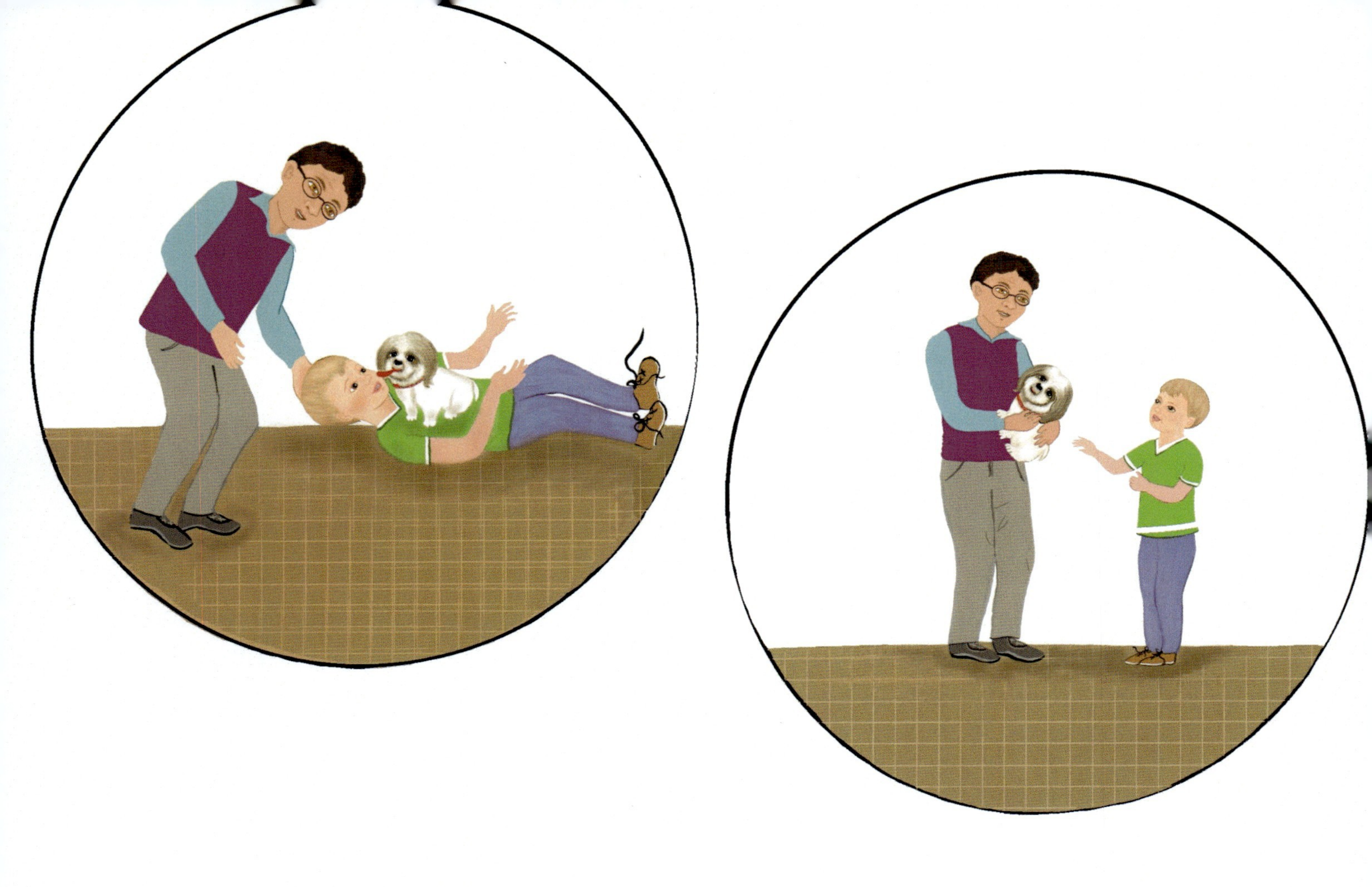

Picking up the little boy and the little tan and white pup, Mr. Chinny Chin Chin handed the dog over to Creed Henry.

The puppy continued to lick the boy's face. Creed Henry quickly bonded with the little puppy.

Laughing he said, "I think I want this one! He really likes me!"

"He sure does," said Mommy and Daddy. "What kind of dog is he?"

"He is a Shih Tzu," Mr. Chinny Chin Chin answered.

"A SHIH TZU! What's a SHIH TZU?" Creed Henry asked giggling.

"A Shih Tzu is a breed of dog that originally came from a far away place called Tibet. Their name, Shih Tzu, means Little Lion."

"I love HIM! I will name him Lion! Said Creed Henry.

Creed Henry held Lion on his lap all the way home. He ran upstairs to his room to show Ruff his new puppy but she was no where to be found. He looked under the bed and in his closet but still could not find Ruff.

"Ruff! Ruff! Come out...I have something to show you!"

He looked all around his room looking for her.

"Where could she be?" Creed Henry asked Lion.

Sadly, Creed Henry sat on top of his bed with Lion. He felt a bump under the covers. At first he thought it was his pillow but then he quickly pulled back his blanket. There she was! Ruff was just sleeping thought the little boy! Creed Henry picked up the stuffed animal trying to get her to talk again.

"Ruff, look! Here is my new puppy. His name is Lion!" Creed Henry said showing Ruff.

Ruff looked the same and smelled the same but she wasn't talking. Lion sniffed the stuffed animal and started to play with Ruff but Ruff didn't move.

"What happened, Ruff? Why aren't you talking anymore?" Asked Creed Henry.

The boy hugged Ruff and told her how much he loved her. He told her all about the Mr. Chinny Chin Chin Puppy Store and how he picked out Lion.

"Well, he really picked me out! He's called a Shih Tzu. I know it's a funny name and you probably are thinking, 'What's a Shih Tzu' just like I asked Mr. Chinny Chin Chin!"

Ruff didn't answer. She laid still next to the boy and Lion on the bed just like a stuffed animal.

"Shih Tzu means little lion. That is why I named him Lion. Do you like his name, Ruff?" Asked Creed Henry.

Ruff still didn't move or talk. Lion decided to lick Ruff's face but she still didn't move!

"Come on, Lion. Let's go for a walk and when we get back, maybe, Ruff will come alive again."

On the walk, Creed Henry started to think that maybe Ruff was never really alive. Maybe, he dreamed the whole thing. Stuffed animals can't talk or move! The more he thought about it the more he convinced himself it was all a dream. Maybe God made him dream about Ruff being alive so he would be patient until his parents allowed him to get a real puppy! Creed Henry knew God shows you things in all different kind of ways. You just have to pay attention to Him.

That night, Creed Henry snuggled close in bed with Lion on one side of him and Ruff on the other.

"Thank you God for this puppy. Thank you for creating him and thank you for creating me so I could have Lion! Oh, and thank you for giving me Ruff to keep me company since I was a baby! Amen and good night!"

Once Creed Henry's eyes were closed, he quickly drifted off to sleep. In his dream he heard, "I was alive in your eyes little boy. I will always be with you in your memories. But you have a real puppy now so I can go back to being your stuffed animal friend. As you grow, you will go through different stages of life. Some stages are for learning, some are for fun, some are for growing up. You have grown up now. Lion is a symbol to remind you that Christians are to be bold and strong like lions. And, yes, even little lions are bold!"

Creed Henry smiled, still half asleep he snuggled close to Lion. In a sleepy voice he said, “I know...I know...”

Lion licked the boy’s face before falling off to sleep. The Shih Tzu, known as the Little Lion, and the little boy lived happily ever after.

The End

Proverbs 28:1: The wicked run away when no one is chasing them, but the godly are as bold as lions.

Printed in the United States
by Baker & Taylor Publisher Services